THE POLITICS OF SAVING THE ENVIRONMENT

THE ENVIRONMENT: *OURS TO SAVE*

THE POLITICS OF SAVING THE ENVIRONMENT

EDITED BY MICHAEL ANDERSON

Britannica® Educational Publishing
IN ASSOCIATION WITH
ROSEN
EDUCATIONAL SERVICES

Published in 2012 by Britannica Educational Publishing
(a trademark of Encyclopædia Britannica, Inc.)
in association with Rosen Educational Services, LLC
29 East 21st Street, New York, NY 10010.

Distributed exclusively by Rosen Educational Services.
For a listing of additional Britannica Educational Publishing titles, call toll free (800) 237-9932.

First Edition

Britannica Educational Publishing
Michael I. Levy: Executive Editor, Encyclopædia Britannica
J.E. Luebering: Director, Core Reference Group, Encyclopædia Britannica
Adam Augustyn: Assistant Manager, Encyclopædia Britannica

Anthony L. Green: Editor, Compton's by Britannica
Michael Anderson: Senior Editor, Compton's by Britannica
Sherman Hollar: Associate Editor, Compton's by Britannica

Marilyn L. Barton: Senior Coordinator, Production Control
Steven Bosco: Director, Editorial Technologies
Lisa S. Braucher: Senior Producer and Data Editor
Yvette Charboneau: Senior Copy Editor
Kathy Nakamura: Manager, Media Acquisition

Rosen Educational Services
Heather M. Moore Niver: Editor
Nelson Sá: Art Director
Cindy Reiman: Photography Manager
Karen Huang: Photo Research
Matthew Cauli: Designer, Cover Design
Introduction by Rick Adair and Heather M. Moore Niver

Library of Congress Cataloging-in-Publication Data

The politics of saving the environment / edited by Michael Anderson.
p. cm.—(The environment: ours to save)
"In association with Britannica Educational Publishing, Rosen Educational Services."
Includes bibliographical references and index.
ISBN 978-1-61530-505-6 (library binding)
1. Environmentalism--Juvenile literature. 2. Environmentalism--Political aspects--Juvenile literature. 3. Environmental policy--Juvenile literature. 4. Environmentalism--United States--Juvenile literature. 5. Environmentalism--Political aspects--United States--Juvenile literature. I. Anderson, Michael (Michael J.), 1972-
GE195.5.P65 2012
337.72—dc22

2010052214

Manufactured in the United States of America

On the cover: (front inset) Activists show their support of the Kyoto Protocol at a protest during the 2010 United Nations Climate Change Conference in Cancun, Mexico. *LatinContent/Getty Images*

Front cover background, back cover, page 3: Solar panels. *Shutterstock.com*

Interior background *Shutterstock.com*

Contents

INTRODUCTION

Mounting evidence suggests that human activities are warming Earth at an alarming rate. Global warming could alter social and economic fabrics around the world as its environmental effects play out. Global warming is among the top concerns of the environmental movement today. However, such an enormous problem is more than individuals can solve. In the end the solution lies with governments, which can change policies and mandate behaviors with a pen stroke. This volume explores the intersection of environmentalism and politics. It introduces the various schools of environmentalism as well as the field of environmental law, which provides a means for carrying out real environmental change. The book also offers an overview of a key factor of the environmental movement—the protection of endangered species.

The modern environmental movement developed in the late 19th century. Early environmental organizations were concerned mainly with nature conservation, wildlife protection, and limiting the pollution that arose from industrial development. The movement included diverse schools of thought.

For example, during the early 1900s, debates raged among conservationists over building a dam on Yosemite National Park's Tuolumne River to provide San Francisco with water. Preservationist members of the conservation movement, advocating the preservation of nature for its own sake, opposed the dam on principle. Utilitarian members of the movement, advocating the wise use of natural resources, supported the project. The preservationists lost; the dam was completed in 1923. However, the debate inspired preservationists to campaign for national park protection, which led to the creation of the National Park Service.

Plitvice Lakes National Park, Croatia. Shutterstock.com

The conservation movement nudged government into the role of nature's steward. In addition to creating the National Park Service, in the late 1800s and early 1900s the federal government established the national forest system and the Forest Service, introduced natural resource management and large-scale irrigation projects, and established a national wildlife refuge system. Theodore Roosevelt, president of the United States from 1901 to 1909, made conservation a cornerstone of his administration.

A population surge following World War II put pressure on undeveloped areas and thus heightened awareness of the strains on nature and raised concerns about air and water pollution, radiation, and pesticide poisoning. Biologist Rachel Carson's best-selling book *Silent Spring* (1962) created worldwide awareness of the dangers of environmental pollution, especially pesticide use. The environmental movement's influence expanded into courtrooms in 1965 when the conservation group Scenic Hudson Preservation Conference successfully challenged New York's utility company, Consolidated Edison, over its plans to build a power plant near the Hudson River. Politicians quickly caught on, and environmentalism became a vital campaign issue in the United States in the late 1960s. In other countries environmentalists made significant political progress beginning in the 1970s and 1980s. "Green" party candidates won national offices in Europe as well as in Australia, New Zealand, Mexico, and Brazil, among other countries.

Endangered species protection is a critical element of environmentalism. Forest destruction, wetland drainage, pollution, pesticides, and other dangers have threatened the survival of plant and animal species worldwide. Elephants are just one high-profile example. They have been reduced to critically low numbers because of uncontrolled killing for their tusks. The International Union for Conservation of Nature (IUCN), the largest conservation organization in the world, publishes information on endangered species worldwide in the IUCN Red List of Threatened Species.

A quick glance at magazine racks or bookshelves confirms that "green" living is part of the public consciousness. Despite this progress, however, environmentalists are hardly complacent, and they continue their efforts in the political realm. They know that for widespread environmental change to take hold, politics must be part of the solution.

CHAPTER 1

Environmentalism: An Overview

The political and intellectual movement called environmentalism seeks to improve and protect the quality of the natural environment. It advocates curtailing or ending human activities that harm the environment. The movement also seeks to change political and economic systems so that human societies can prosper without causing pollution and other environmental damage.

The term *environment* is broad, as it refers to all the natural world. In various ways, environmentalists call for protecting or improving the quality of the air, the water, and the land, including the conservation of the soil and important natural areas such as rainforests and wetlands. Environmentalists are also concerned with protecting the biosphere, which consists of the animals, plants, and other living things and the ecosystems in which they live.

Environmentalists aim to preserve and care for air, water, and land, as well as the animals, plants, and other living things that live there. **Shutterstock.com**

Goals and Methods

The goals and methods of different environmentalists are quite varied. For example, some focus on raising public awareness of the need to "reduce, reuse, and recycle" materials, to cut back on the resources consumed in making, packaging, and transporting consumer products. Others work to enact local, national, or international laws that protect the environment, such as by requiring that motor vehicles meet certain fuel efficiency and emissions standards, creating nature reserves, banning the killing of endangered species, or regulating the chemicals that businesses can emit into the air and water. Some environmentalists organize various kinds of protest actions to draw attention to or to disrupt activities by corporations and governments that harm the environment. Others seek to establish alternative communities that live in closer harmony with nature.

Despite the diversity of the movement, most environmentalists agree on four general principles: protection of the environment, democracy, social justice, and nonviolence. However, a few individuals and groups believe that violence in the name of environmentalism is justified if it is committed against

Many environmentalists suggest recycling plastics, paper, and metals to preserve the environment. **Shutterstock.com**

businesses that damage the environment or that kill or abuse animals for profit, such as mining and logging companies and the makers of fur coats. Critics of this practice, many of whom are not themselves environmentalists, have referred to it as "ecoterrorism."

Two Basic Approaches

In many cases environmentalists want protection of the natural world to directly improve or maintain human health and well-being. However, many believe that the environment should also be protected in other cases. They claim that living things other than humans, and the natural environment as a whole, should also be taken into account when people reason about the morality of political, economic, and social policies.

Environmentalists are often divided into two intellectual camps: those whose thinking about the environment is anthropocentric, or "human-centered," and those whose thinking is biocentric, or "life-centered." This division has also been described as "shallow" ecology versus "deep" ecology. The division between these two basic approaches played a central role in the development of environmental thought in the late 20th century.

Anthropocentric Schools of Thought

Anthropocentric approaches focus on the negative effects that environmental damage has on human beings, including harm to human health and quality of life. They also tend to think of the value of the natural environment in terms of its usefulness to humans.

According to this approach, for example, the problem with polluting the ocean or depleting the ozone layer is that doing so ultimately harms human beings, who use the ocean as a source of food and rely on the ozone layer for protection against ultraviolet radiation from the Sun.

Apocalyptic Environmentalism

The vision of the environmental movement of the 1960s and early '70s was generally pessimistic, reflecting a belief that Earth's long-term prospects were bleak. Apocalyptic, or "survivalist," environmentalism stressed the possible destruction of the planet. Works such as Rachel Carson's *Silent Spring* (1962) and Paul Ehrlich's *The Population Bomb* (1968) suggested that the natural environment was reaching the limits of what it could sustain. Influenced by such books, some environmentalists began to call for increasing the powers of central governments to limit human activities thought to be environmentally harmful. Robert Heilbroner's *An Inquiry into the Human Prospect* (1974), for example, argued that human survival ultimately required the sacrifice of human freedom.

Rachel Carson

Drawing on her childhood fascination with wildlife and the sea, American biologist Rachel Carson became a scientific writer whose works appeal to a wide range of readers. Her enchanting book *The Sea Around Us*, published in 1951, was a best-seller and the winner of a National Book Award. Her prophetic work *Silent Spring* (1962), about the dangers of pesticides in the food chain, created worldwide awareness of the dangers of pollution.

Rachel Louise Carson was born on May 27, 1907, in Springdale, Pa. She did her undergraduate work at the Pennsylvania College for Women, where she received her B.A. in 1929. She then went on to earn an M.A. from Johns Hopkins University in 1932. From 1931 to 1936 she taught zoology at the University of Maryland. During this period she also taught in the Johns Hopkins summer school and studied at the Marine Biological Laboratory in Woods Hole, Mass.

Carson accepted a position in 1936 as an aquatic biologist with the United States Bureau of Fisheries (from 1940 called the U.S. Fish and Wildlife Service). She would hold this government post for the next 16 years. From 1949 to 1952 she served as editor in chief of the Fish and Wildlife Service's publications. By that time Carson had become widely known as a science writer. Her first three books were about sea life: *Under the Sea-Wind* (1941), *The Sea Around Us*, and *The Edge of the Sea* (1955) displayed Carson's remarkable talent for combining scientific observation with elegant and lyrical prose descriptions.

After the publication of *The Edge of the Sea*, Carson spent much of the next five years conducting research for *Silent Spring*. The book, which detailed the harmful effects that pesticides such as DDT had on the environment—and particularly on wildlife—became her second best-seller and today is regarded as a landmark work in the history of the modern environmental movement. Carson died on April 14, 1964.

Other viewpoints, such as those presented in Julian Simon and Herman Kahn's *The Resourceful Earth* (1984), have emphasized humanity's ability to find or invent substitutes for resources that were scarce and in danger of being exhausted.

Emancipatory Environmentalism

Beginning in the 1970s, many environmentalists began to develop strategies for limiting environmental damage through recycling, the use of alternative-energy technologies, and increasing government regulation of industries that harm the environment. They have

By encouraging the use of alternative-energy strategies, such as solar panels, environmentalists can promote a constructive, ethical approach. **Lester Lefkowitz/Stone/Getty Images**

also sought to increase popular participation in economic planning, such as by introducing citizen representation on the boards of major corporations and by allowing the public to vote on environmentally sensitive decisions by businesses and government. In contrast to apocalyptic environmentalism, so-called "emancipatory" environmentalism has taken a more positive and practical approach. One element of this approach has been to promote an ethic of stewardship, or responsible management, of the environment.

Some forms of emancipatory environmentalism have emphasized the development of small-scale farms and industries that would be more closely integrated with the natural processes of the surrounding environment. Prominent environmentalists advocating this approach included American ecologist Barry Commoner and German-born British economist Ernst Schumacher. Such environmentalists also encourage the use of renewable resources (those that can be replenished comparatively quickly, easily, and inexpensively), such as wind and solar power, rather than nonrenewable resources, such as fossil fuels. They also advocate organic farming, which uses biological methods of fertilization and pest control rather than chemical fertilizers and pesticides. The emancipatory approach was evoked through the 1990s in the popular slogan, "think globally, act locally."

Biocentric Schools of Thought

Proponents of biocentrism claim that it is wrong to treat the environment merely as a resource to be exploited for human purposes.

They hold that nature is valuable for its own sake. Polluting the ocean or depleting the ozone layer would be wrong, therefore, even if the ocean or the ozone layer did not benefit human beings in any way. Advocates of biocentrism believe that anthropocentric approaches have been responsible for centuries of environmental destruction.

Social Ecology

An emphasis on small-scale economic structures is also a feature of the school of thought known as social ecology. Social ecologists trace the causes of environmental damage to what they consider to be the unfair distribution of political and economic power in society. They see this problem as characteristic of modern capitalist societies, in which power is centralized in large government agencies or private businesses that are not accountable to the people who work in them or who are affected by them. They argue that the most environmentally beneficial political and economic system is one based on decentralized, small-scale communities and systems of production. A major proponent of social ecology was the American environmental anarchist Murray Bookchin.

DEEP ECOLOGY

A more radical doctrine, known as deep ecology, also distrusts capitalism and favors decentralization. Deep ecologists claim that humans need to regain a "spiritual" relationship with nonhuman nature. They believe that people should reflect on the interconnectedness of all organisms—including humans—in the natural environment and cultivate in themselves a sympathy for nonhuman nature. By doing this, they argue, humans can develop an environmental consciousness and a feeling of environmental solidarity. Some more extreme forms of deep ecology have been strongly criticized, however, as "antihumanist," because they imply that one should oppose famine relief and immigration and accept the large-scale losses of life that have been caused by HIV/AIDS and other epidemics.

ANIMAL RIGHTS

A belief in the intrinsic value of nature was fundamental to the development of the animal-rights movement. The movement was strongly influenced by works such as Peter Singer's *Animal Liberation* (1977) and

Arne Næss, a Norwegian philosopher and environmentalist, was one of the original deep ecologists. Erlend Aas/AFP/Getty Images

Tom Regan's *The Case for Animal Rights* (1983). Animal-rights approaches go beyond a concern with cruelty to animals to demand an end to all forms of animal exploitation. For example, many animal-rights activists oppose the use of animals in scientific and medical experiments and as sources of food, clothing, and entertainment (such as in circuses, rodeos, and races).

Ecofeminism

The possibility of a spiritual relationship with nature has also been a concern of ecofeminism. Ecofeminists assert that there is a connection between the destruction of nature by humans and the oppression of women by men. Both, they argue, arise from political viewpoints and social practices in which both women and nature are treated as objects to be owned or controlled. Ecofeminists aim to establish a central role for women in the pursuit of an environmentally sound and socially just society. They hold that the relationship between nature and women is more intimate and more "spiritual" than the relationship between nature and men.

CHAPTER 2
History of the Environmental Movement

Concern for the effect on human life of problems such as air and water pollution dates to at least Roman times. Soil conservation was practiced in China, India, and Peru as early as 2,000 years ago. In general, however, such concerns did not give rise to public activism.

Early Environmentalism

The contemporary environmental movement developed in the late 19th century. It arose primarily from concerns about the protection of the countryside in Europe and of the wilderness in the United States and the health consequences of pollution during the Industrial Revolution. The dominant political philosophy of the time was liberalism. It held that all social problems, including environmental ones, could and should be solved through the free market—the exchange of goods and services in

John Muir (right) with President Theodore Roosevelt. MPI/Archive Photos/Getty Images

the economy without any government regulation. However, most early environmentalists believed that government rather than the market should be responsible for protecting the environment and ensuring the conservation of resources.

In the United States a more strongly biocentric approach was advocated by the naturalist John Muir (1838–1914), founder of the Sierra Club, and Aldo Leopold (1887–1948), a professor of wildlife management. Leopold introduced the concept of a "land ethic." According to him, humans needed to stop being conquerors of nature and to start being "citizens" of nature.

Environmental organizations established from the late 19th to the mid-20th century were primarily middle-class groups concerned with nature conservation, wildlife protection, and limiting the pollution that arose from industrial development and urbanization. Their emphasis was typically on lobbying, or trying to influence the decisions of legislators and government policy makers. In addition, various scientific organizations were concerned with natural history and the biological aspects of conservation efforts.

JOHN MUIR

American naturalist, explorer, and writer John Muir played a key role in the expansion of the United States national park system. In 1903 he made a camping trip in Yosemite with President Theodore Roosevelt, who absorbed Muir's enthusiasm for nature. During the remainder of Roosevelt's presidency, 148 million acres (60 million hectares) were set aside as national forests; 16 national monuments, including Muir Woods in California, were established; and the number of national parks doubled.

John Muir was born on April 21, 1838, in Dunbar, Scotland. In 1849 the family immigrated to the United States and settled on a farm near Portage, Wis. Muir entered the University of Wisconsin but left without a degree because he studied only the subjects that interested him—chemistry, geology, and botany.

In 1867, after an injury threatened blindness, Muir walked from Indianapolis, where he had worked in a wagon factory, all the way to the Gulf of Mexico. For six years he lived alone in the Yosemite Valley, exploring the glaciers and forests of the Sierra Nevada. In Alaska he discovered Glacier Bay and the great glacier named for him.

After his marriage in 1880 he devoted ten years to his California fruit ranch. His gift for growing plants and for developing new varieties of fruits and flowers brought him success and the freedom to travel and write. Muir was largely responsible for the establishment of Sequoia and Yosemite national parks in 1890. In 1892 he founded the Sierra Club, an organization devoted to protecting the environment. He served as its first president, a position he held until his death. He died in Los Angeles on Dec. 24, 1914.

The Greens

Beginning in the 1960s, environmentalists began to establish activist organizations and political parties. The early activities of the "green" movement, as environmentalism came to be called, involved protest actions designed to obstruct and to draw attention to environmentally harmful policies and projects. Other activities included public education campaigns and conventional lobbying of policy makers and political representatives. The movement also attempted to set public examples to increase awareness of environmental issues. Such projects included recycling and green consumerism, or "buying green," which means choosing products whose production, packaging, distribution, use, and disposal cause less harm to the environment than similar products.

The political strategies of the green movement included forming its own political parties and nominating candidates to run for political office. Through these parties, the movement sought to make the environment a central concern of public policy and to render the institutions of government more democratic and accountable.

The First Green Parties

The world's first green parties were founded in the early 1970s in New Zealand and Tasmania, Australia. The first explicitly green member of a national legislature was elected in Switzerland in 1979. Later, in 1981, four greens won legislative seats in Belgium. Green parties were established in the former Soviet bloc, where they were instrumental in the collapse of some communist regimes. Green parties were also formed in some developing countries in Asia, South America, and Africa.

The most successful environmental party was the German Green party, founded in West Germany in 1980. In federal elections just three years later, the party won representation in the country's parliament. In 1998 it formed a coalition government of a united

Germany with the Social Democratic party, and the party's leader, Joschka Fischer, was appointed the country's foreign minister.

Electoral Victories

In the late 20th and early 21st centuries, green party candidates won election to national parliaments in a number of countries—especially in Europe but also in such countries as Australia, New Zealand, Mexico, and Brazil—and some became government ministers. Green parties even claimed the office of mayor in European capital cities such as Dublin and Rome in the mid-1990s. In other places, including the United States, green party candidates were elected mayor of smaller cities or to other local offices.

International Environmental Movement

By the late 1980s environmentalism had become a global as well as a national political force. Some environmental nongovernmental organizations—for example, Greenpeace, Friends of the Earth, and the World Wildlife Fund—established a significant international presence. Such organizations had offices

Organizations such as Greenpeace broadcast their environmental message more widely by establishing an international presence. **Mike Clarke/AFP/Getty Images**

throughout the world and international headquarters to coordinate lobbying campaigns and to serve as information centers for their national affiliate organizations.

Through its international activism, the environmental movement has influenced the agenda of international politics. Few international environmental agreements were in force before the 1960s. However, since the 1972 United Nations Conference on the Human Environment in Stockholm, Sweden, there have been international agreements on most aspects of environmental protection. International agreements have also been made about practices that have environmental consequences, such as the trade in endangered species, the management of hazardous waste (especially nuclear waste), and armed conflict. In 1992 the United Nations Conference on Environment and Development (the "Earth Summit") in Rio de Janeiro, Brazil, was attended by some 180 countries and various business groups, nongovernmental organizations, and the media. An important international treaty called the Kyoto Protocol was adopted in 1997 and went into effect in 2005. Through this treaty, many countries agreed to reduce by specific amounts their emissions of certain gases that cause global warming.

At the beginning of the 21st century, the environmental movement combined the traditional concerns of conservation, preservation, and pollution with more contemporary concerns such as the environmental consequences of tourism and trade. The short- and long-term effects of global warming also became more of a concern.

ENVIRONMENTAL PROTECTION IN THE UNITED STATES

As mentioned earlier, conservation in the United States began as a movement in the late 19th century to save the country's wilderness areas, especially its vanishing forests. Most early environmentalists believed that government should be charged with protecting the environment and ensuring the conservation of resources.

EARLY CONSERVATION EFFORTS

Gifford Pinchot, the head of the United States Forest Service from 1898 to 1910, was an early conservationist. He strongly influenced President Theodore Roosevelt, who established the National Conservation Commission. Some 234 million acres (95 million hectares) of government-owned timber, coal, oil, and phosphate lands were set apart as public lands, never to be sold to private interests.

During President Franklin D. Roosevelt's first term, with a severe drought in the Plains states, reforestation and erosion control were undertaken by the Civilian Conservation Corps and the Soil Conservation Service.

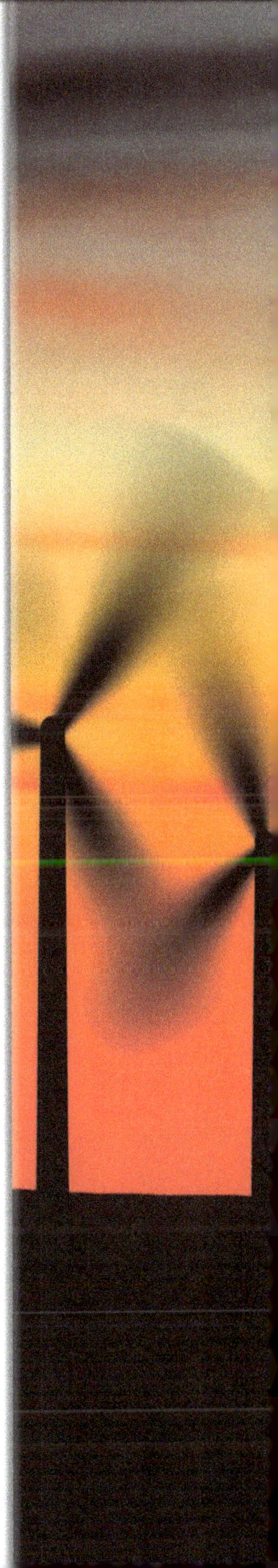

The government took over abandoned and nonproductive farms, and many acres were reforested and set aside as game reserves. The Taylor Grazing Act of 1934 regulated livestock grazing on public lands to prevent overgrazing and soil deterioration.

Under President Harry S. Truman, a national program was established to control water pollution. Later legislation required states to set and enforce standards to maintain clean natural waters.

Endangered Species Policy

Efforts to save native wildlife from extinction were aided by management programs provided in the Endangered Species Preservation Act of 1966. Beginning in 1969 the importation of endangered species and the interstate shipment of illegally captured wildlife were prohibited. Thus the pet, fur, and hide markets for native and foreign species facing potential extinction were outlawed.

Environmental Protection Agency

The National Environmental Policy Act of 1969, a far-reaching conservation measure, was supported by President Richard M.

The giant otter of South America has been widely hunted and is now an endangered species. **Encyclopædia Britannica, Inc.**

Nixon. It emphasized recycling of nonrenewable resources and advocated attempts to equalize population and resource use. In 1970 the Environmental Protection Agency (EPA) was formed to establish standards of environmental quality. Since then the EPA has been responsible for enforcing several major statutes, including such landmark environmental laws as the Clean Air Act of 1970 and what became known as the Clean Water Act of 1972, to protect the environment from air

The Environmental Protection Agency, located in Washington, D.C. **Comstock/Thinkstock**

and water pollution. These acts have subsequently been amended and additional ones passed, but this basic framework of environmental protections remains in place.

RECENT APPROACHES

Various presidential administrations in the late 20th and early 21st century took

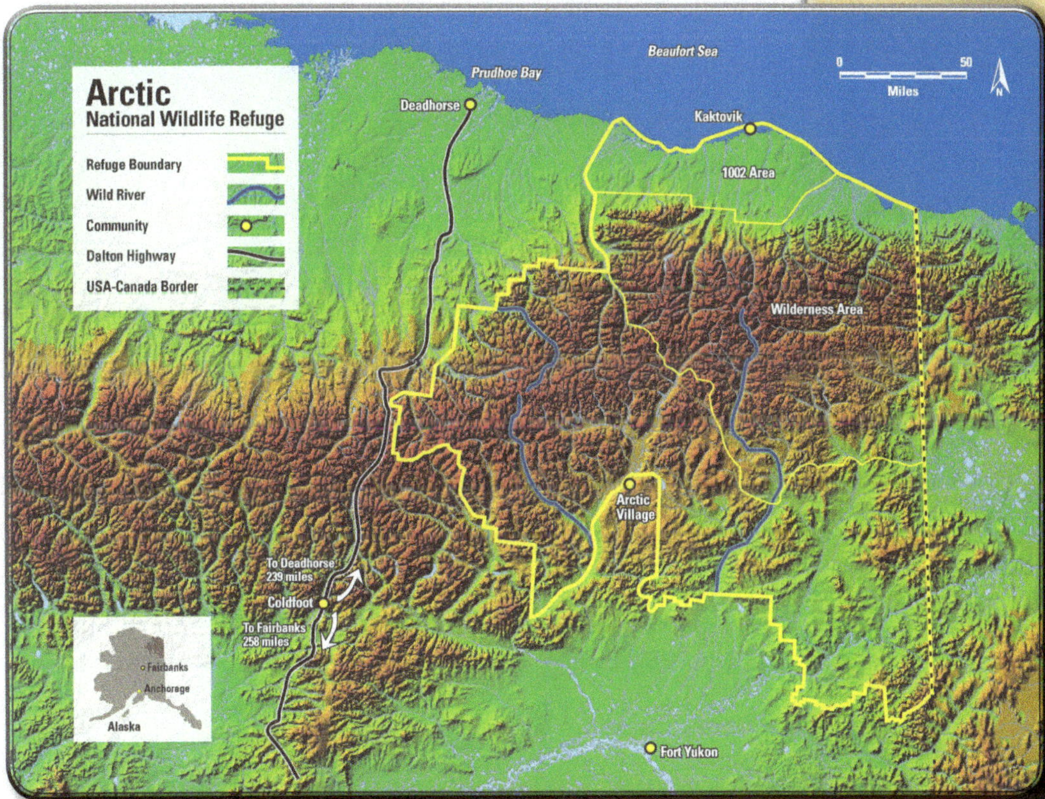

The Arctic National Wildlife Refuge. Getty Images

different approaches toward the environment, with some favoring land development, resource exploitation, and deregulation of industries over conservation of wildlife and natural ecosystems and protections against environmental pollution. Contentious issues included whether to prohibit new road construction in certain national forests to protect them from excessive timbering, whether to open large areas of key wildlife habitat in the Arctic National Wildlife Refuge to oil drilling, and whether to require automobiles to meet stricter fuel-efficiency standards.

CHAPTER 3
An Introduction to Environmental Law

The success of environmentalists' efforts is often measured in terms of the laws that they help create. The vast field of environmental law encompasses the principles and policies enacted by local, national, and international entities to regulate human treatment of the nonhuman world. The field covers a broad range of topics in diverse legal settings, such as state bottle-return laws in the United States, regulatory standards for emissions from coal-fired power plants in Germany, and international treaties for the protection of biological diversity and the ozonosphere. During the late 20th century, environmental law developed from a modest outgrowth of the law of public health regulations into an almost universally recognized independent field protecting both human health and nonhuman nature.

Levels of Environmental Law

Environmental law exists at many levels and is only partly established by international

State bottle-return laws in the United States are an example of environmental regulations in action. iStockphoto/Thinkstock

declarations, conventions, and treaties. The bulk of environmental law is statutory—that is, encompassed in the enactments of legislative bodies—and regulatory—that is, generated by agencies charged by governments with protection of the environment.

Constitutional Guarantees

Many countries have included some right to environmental quality in their national constitutions. Since 1994, for example, environmental protection has been enshrined in the German Grundgesetz ("Basic Law"), which now states that the government must protect for "future generations the natural

The German Grundgesetz ("Basic Law") maintains that the government must protect the environment for the sake of future generations. **Shutterstock.com**

foundations of life." Similarly, the Chinese constitution declares that the state "ensures the rational use of natural resources and protects rare animals and plants." The South African constitution recognizes a right to "an environment that is not harmful to health or well-being; and to have the environment protected, for the benefit of present and future generations." Bulgaria's constitution provides for a "right to a healthy and favourable environment, consistent with stipulated standards and regulations." The Chilean constitution contains a "right to live in an environment free from contamination."

Court Decisions

Much environmental law also is embodied in the decisions of international, national, and local courts. Some of it is manifested in arbitrated decisions, such as the Trail Smelter arbitration (1941), which enjoined the operation of a smelter located in British Columbia, Canada, near the international border with the U.S. state of Washington and held that "no State has the right to use or permit the use of its territory in such a manner as to cause injury by fumes in or to the territory of another or the properties or persons therein." Some environmental law also appears in the decisions of national courts. For example, in *Scenic Hudson Preservation Conference v. Federal Power Commission* (1965), a U.S. federal appeals court voided a license granted by the Federal Power Commission for the construction of an environmentally damaging pumped-storage hydroelectric

A ruling by the California Supreme Court in 1976 dramatically limited how much water the city of Los Angeles could redirect from Mono Lake. **Shutterstock.com**

plant (that is, a plant that would pump water from a lower to an upper reservoir) in an area of stunning natural beauty, demonstrating that the decisions of federal agencies could be successfully challenged in the courts. Significant local decisions included *National Audubon Society v. Superior Court* (1976), in which the California Supreme Court dramatically limited the ability of the Los Angeles to divert water that might otherwise fill Mono Lake in California's eastern desert.

Current Trends and Prospects

Although numerous international environmental treaties have been concluded, effective agreements remain difficult to achieve for a variety of reasons. Because environmental problems ignore political boundaries, they can be adequately addressed only with the cooperation of numerous governments, among which there may be serious disagreements on important points of environmental policy. Furthermore, because the measures necessary to address environmental problems typically result in social and economic hardships in the countries that adopt them, many countries, particularly in the developing world, have been reluctant to enter into environmental treaties.

Many areas of international environmental law remain underdeveloped. Although international agreements have helped make the laws and regulations applicable to some types of environmentally harmful activity more or less consistent in different countries, those applicable to other such activities can dramatically differ. Because in most cases the damage caused by environmentally harmful activities cannot be contained within national boundaries, the lack of consistency in the law has led to situations in which activities that are legal in some countries result in illegal or otherwise unacceptable levels of environmental damage in neighboring countries. Since the 1970s a growing number of environmental treaties have incorporated provisions designed to encourage their adoption by developing countries. Such measures include financial cooperation, technology transfer, and differential implementation schedules and obligations.

Enforcement Efforts

The greatest challenge to the effectiveness of environmental treaties is compliance. Although treaties can attempt to enforce compliance through mechanisms such as sanctions, these measures are usually only somewhat useful. In part this is because countries may be unwilling or unable to impose the sanctions called for by the treaty. In general, the threat of sanctions is less important to most countries than the possibility that by violating their international obligations they risk losing their good standing in the international community.

Enforcement mechanisms other than sanctions have been difficult to establish, usually because they would require countries to cede significant aspects of their national sovereignty to foreign or international organizations. In most agreements, therefore, enforcement is treated as a domestic issue. This approach effectively allows each country to define compliance in a way that best serves its national interest. Despite this difficulty, international environmental treaties and agreements are likely to grow in importance as international environmental problems become more severe.

With virtually no environmental law enforcement, many maquiladoras have been free to pollute surrounding areas. **Stephen Ferry/ Getty Images**

Cross-Border Challenges

The problem of enforcement across international borders became particularly critical with the adoption of free trade agreements beginning in the early 1990s. The North American Free Trade Agreement (NAFTA), for example, resulted in the creation of large numbers of maquiladoras—factories jointly owned by U.S. and Mexican corporations and

North American Free Trade Agreement (NAFTA)

The North American Free Trade Agreement (NAFTA) was signed by the United States, Canada, and Mexico in 1992, and it took effect in 1994. NAFTA called for elimination of all trade barriers between the three countries over a 15-year period. It also granted U.S. and Canadian companies access to certain Mexican markets and incorporated agreements on labor and the environment.

One result of NAFTA was a proliferation of maquiladoras. These factories import parts duty-free, assemble them, and export the finished products, including motor vehicles, electronics, and furniture. American companies set up the maquiladoras in Mexico to take advantage of low labor costs and more relaxed environmental laws. In the 1990s, however, some maquiladoras were criticized for poor working conditions and extremely long workweeks as well as for contributing to environmental pollution.

operated in Mexico—inside a zone extending 60 miles (100 kilometers) south from the U.S.-Mexican border. Because Mexico's government lacked both the resources and the political will to enforce the country's environmental laws, the maquiladoras were able to pollute surrounding areas with relative freedom, often dumping hazardous wastes on the ground or directly into waterways, where they were carried into U.S. territory. Prior to NAFTA's adoption in 1992, the prospect of problems such as these led negotiators to append a so-called "side agreement" to the treaty, which pledged environmental cooperation between the signatory states. Meanwhile, European concerns about the apparent connection between free trade agreements and environmental degradation fueled opposition to the Maastricht Treaty, which created the European Union and expanded its jurisdiction.

CHAPTER 4
HISTORY OF ENVIRONMENTAL LAW

Throughout history national governments have passed occasional laws to protect human health from environmental contamination. About AD 80 the Senate of Rome passed legislation to protect the city's supply of clean water for drinking and bathing. In the 14th century, England prohibited both the burning of coal in London and the disposal of waste into waterways. In 1681 the Quaker leader of the English colony of Pennsylvania, William Penn, ordered that one acre of forest be preserved for every five acres cleared for settlement. In the following century, Benjamin Franklin led various campaigns to curtail the dumping of waste. In the midst of the Industrial Revolution, in the 19th century, the British government passed regulations to reduce the harmful effects of coal burning and chemical manufacture on public health and the environment.

Benjamin Franklin. **Stock Montage/Archive Photos/Getty Images**

Early International Agreements

Prior to the 20th century, there were few international environmental agreements. The accords that were reached focused primarily on boundary waters, navigation, and fishing rights along shared waterways and ignored pollution and other ecological issues. In the early 20th century, conventions to protect commercially valuable species were reached, including the Convention for the Protection of Birds Useful to Agriculture (1902), signed by 12 European governments; the Convention for the Preservation and Protection of Fur Seals (1911), concluded by the United States, Japan, Russia, and the United Kingdom; and the Convention for the Protection of Migratory Birds (1916), adopted by the United States and the United Kingdom (on behalf of Canada) and later extended to Mexico in 1936.

In the 1930s Belgium, Egypt, Italy, Portugal, South Africa, Sudan, and the United Kingdom adopted the Convention Relative to the Preservation of Fauna and Flora in their Natural State, which committed those countries to preserve natural fauna and flora in Africa by means of national parks

Fur seals were granted protection by the United States, Japan, Russia, and the United Kingdom in 1911. Joel Sartore/National Geographic Image Collection/Getty Images

and reserves. Spain and France signed the convention but never ratified it, and Tanzania formally adopted it in 1962. India, which consented to the agreement in 1939, was subject to the sections of the document prohibiting "trophies" made from any animal mentioned in the annex.

A Surge in National Laws

Beginning in the 1960s, environmentalism became an important political and intellectual movement in the West. In the United States the publication of biologist Rachel Carson's *Silent Spring* (1962), a passionate and persuasive examination of chlorinated hydrocarbon pesticides and the environmental damage caused by their use, led to a reconsideration of a much broader range of actual and potential environmental hazards. In the following decades the U.S. government passed an extraordinary number of environmental laws—including acts addressing solid-waste disposal, air and water pollution, and the protection of endangered species—and created an Environmental Protection Agency to monitor compliance with them. These new environmental laws dramatically increased the national government's role in

Rachel Carson. Alfred Eisenstaedt/Time & Life Pictures/Getty Images

an area previously left primarily to state and local regulation.

In Japan rapid reindustrialization after World War II was accompanied by the indiscriminate release of industrial chemicals into the human food chain in certain areas. In the city of Minamata, for example, large numbers of people suffered mercury poisoning after eating fish that had been contaminated with industrial wastes. By the early 1960s, the Japanese government had begun to consider a comprehensive pollution-control policy, and in 1967 Japan enacted the world's first such overarching law, the Basic Law for Environmental Pollution Control. Not until the end of the 20th century was Minamata declared mercury-free.

Thirty-four countries in 1971 adopted the Convention on Wetlands of International Importance Especially as Waterfowl Habitat, generally known as the Ramsar Convention for the city in Iran in which it was signed. The agreement, which entered into force in 1975, now has nearly 100 parties. It required all countries to designate at least one protected wetland area, and it recognized the important role of wetlands in maintaining the ecological equilibrium.

United Nations Environment Programme

Following the United Nations (UN) Conference on the Human Environment, held in Stockholm in 1972, the UN established the United Nations Environment Programme (UNEP) as the world's principal international environmental organization. Although UNEP oversees many modern-day agreements, it has little power to impose or enforce sanctions on noncomplying parties. Nevertheless, a series of important conventions arose directly from the conference, including the London Convention on the Prevention of Pollution by Dumping of Wastes or Other Matter (1972) and the Convention on International Trade in Endangered Species (1973).

Environmental Protection in Europe

Until the Stockholm conference, European countries generally had been slow to enact legal standards for environmental protection—though there had been some exceptions, such as the passage of the conservationist Countryside Act in the United Kingdom in 1968. In October 1972, only a few months after the UN conference, the leaders of the European Community (EC) declared that the goal of economic expansion had to be balanced with the need to protect the environment. In the following year the European Commission, the EC's executive branch, produced its first Environmental Action Programme, and

When acid rain damaged German forests, the public rallied for environmental regulations. **Shutterstock.com**

since that time European countries have been at the forefront of environmental policy making. In Germany, for example, public attitudes toward environmental protection changed dramatically in the early 1980s, when it became known that many German forests were being destroyed by acid rain. The environmentalist German Green party, founded in 1980, won representation in the Bundestag (national parliament) for the first time in 1983 and since then has campaigned for stricter environmental regulations. By the end of the 20th century the party had joined a coalition government and was responsible for developing and implementing Germany's extensive environmental policies. As a group, Germany, The Netherlands, and Denmark—the so-called "green troika"—established themselves as leading innovators in environmental law.

EFFECTS OF THE CHERNOBYL DISASTER

During the 1980s the "transboundary effects" of environmental pollution in individual countries spurred negotiations on several international environmental conventions. The effects of the 1986 accident at the nuclear power plant at Chernobyl in Ukraine (then part of the Soviet Union) were especially significant. European countries in the pollution's downwind path were forced to adopt measures to restrict their populations' consumption of water, milk, meat, and vegetables. In Austria traces of radiation were found in cow's milk as well as in human breast milk. As a direct result of the Chernobyl disaster, two international agreements—the Convention on Early Notification of a Nuclear Accident and the Convention on Assistance in the Case of Nuclear Accident or Radiological Emergency, both adopted in 1986—were rapidly drafted to ensure notification and assistance in the event of a nuclear accident. In the following decade a Convention on Nuclear Safety (1994) established incentives for countries to adopt basic standards for the safe operation of land-based nuclear power plants.

Flexibility in Environmental Laws

There are often conflicting data about the environmental impact of human activities, and scientific uncertainty often has complicated the drafting and implementation of environmental laws and regulations, particularly for international conferences attempting to develop universal standards. Consequently, such laws and regulations usually are designed to be flexible enough to accommodate changes in scientific understanding and technological capacity. The Vienna Convention for the Protection of the Ozone Layer (1985), for example, did not specify the measures that signatory states were required to adopt to protect human health and the environment from the effects of ozone depletion, nor did it mention any substances that were thought to damage the ozone layer. Similarly, the Framework Convention on Climate Change, or Global Warming Convention, adopted by 178 countries meeting in Rio de Janeiro at the 1992 United Nations Conference on Environment and Development (popularly known as the "Earth Summit"), did not set binding targets for reducing the emission of the "greenhouse" gases thought to cause global warming.

Global Warming Policy

The Intergovernmental Panel on Climate Change was established by the World Meteorological Organization and UNEP

Kyoto Protocol

The Kyoto Protocol, adopted in 1997, called on developed countries to reduce their emissions of six greenhouse gases. The overall goal was a reduction of 5.2 percent below 1990 levels between the years 2008 and 2012. The agreement was ratified and took effect in 2005.

The Kyoto Protocol allowed participating countries to use emissions trading to meet their emissions targets. Its market mechanisms included the sale of "emission reduction units," which are earned when a developed country reduces its emissions below its commitment level, to developed countries that have failed to achieve their emission targets. Developed countries could earn additional emission reduction units by financing energy-efficient projects (for example, clean-development mechanisms) in developing countries. Since its adoption, the protocol has encountered stiff opposition from some countries, particularly the United States, which has failed to ratify it.

to study changes in Earth's temperature. In 1995 the panel concluded that "the balance of evidence suggests a discernible human influence on global climate." Although cited by environmentalists as final proof of the reality of global warming, the report was faulted by some critics for relying on insufficient data, overstating the environmental impact of global warming, and using unrealistic models of climate change. Two years later in Kyoto, Japan, a conference of signatories to the Framework Convention on Climate Change adopted the Kyoto Protocol, which featured binding emission targets for developed countries.

CHAPTER 5
Endangered Species

Although there were about 65,000 black rhinoceroses in the world in 1970, at the start of the 21st century there were fewer than 3,000 left. Even rarer was the mandrinette, a shrub from Mauritius with bright red flowers. Fewer than 50 of the plants were known in the wild. The black rhinoceros and the mandrinette are endangered species: they face a high risk of extinction throughout all or a significant portion of their range. An extinct species is one that has completely died out; living individuals of its kind no longer exist. By 2006 the International Union for Conservation of Nature and Natural Resources (IUCN) estimated that more than 16,000 species of animals and plants around the world were threatened with extinction. The protection of endangered species is a key component of the environmental movement.

The black rhinoceros (Diceros bicornis) is listed by the IUCN as critically endangered. **Encyclopædia Britannica, Inc.**

CAUSES OF ENDANGERMENT

Plants and animals have become extinct and new species have evolved since life on Earth began. Preliterate human cultures may have caused the extinction of some species, but the primary causes for species to become extinct were natural ones. Major environmental changes resulted in the eventual disappearance of species unable to adapt to new conditions. Well-known natural extinctions include that of the dinosaurs and many other species represented in the fossil record.

Natural forces are still at work, but human activities cause most of the rapid and widespread environmental changes that affect plants and animals today. Many species have been unable to make the biological adjustments necessary for survival. Thus more species than ever before are threatened with extinction.

Destruction of forests, draining of wetlands, and pollution are environmental

The Tasmanian wolf is presumed extinct. The last known living specimen died in a private zoo in Hobart, Australia, in 1936. **Encyclopædia Britannica, Inc.**

changes that may eliminate species in an area. Some herbicides and pesticides can severely affect certain species. Many species have small geographic ranges, so habitat alteration may eliminate them entirely. The logging of tropical forests, with their tremendous diversity of species having specialized requirements, has caused a steady increase in the extinction rate. Excessive hunting and trapping for commercial purposes also cause major problems. Elephants have been reduced to critically low numbers because of uncontrolled killing for their tusks, which are used to make ivory piano keys, jewelry, and other art objects. Plants also can be reduced to near extinction levels by extensive collecting. Many cactus species of the arid southwestern United States are now legally protected by state laws to prevent their removal.

Sneed Pincushion Cactus
(*Coryphantha sneedii sneedii*)

The Sneed pincushion cactus is an endangered plant species. **Encyclopædia Britannica, Inc.**

The planned or accidental introduction of exotic species to a region can also lead to extinction. An introduced species often has no natural enemies to control its spread, and native species may have no natural protection against it. The introduction of the fungus that causes Dutch elm disease to North America, mongooses to Jamaica, and pigs to Hawaii resulted in the loss of native species that had inadequate defenses.

Protection

Only since the 19th century has there been international concern about the plight of species in their natural environments. In earlier times, when human population sizes were small and modern technology was developing, the effects of human activities on natural populations seldom seemed significant. Protection of animal species on an international scale was initiated as early as 1916 with the Migratory Bird Treaty between the United States, Great Britain, Canada, and later Mexico.

A far-reaching wildlife conservation measure came from a United States–hosted conference in 1973 that resulted in an international treaty known as CITES—the

Convention on International Trade in Endangered Species of Wild Flora and Fauna (CITES)

The Convention on International Trade in Endangered Species of Wild Flora and Fauna, or CITES, sorts more than 5,000 animal and 28,000 plant species into three categories, which are associated with its three appendixes. Appendix I lists the species in danger of extinction. It also prohibits outright the commercial trade of these species, but some can be traded in extraordinary situations for scientific or educational reasons. In contrast, Appendix II lists particular plants and animals that are less threatened but still require stringent controls. Appendix III lists species that are protected in at least one country that has petitioned other countries for help in controlling international trade in that species.

Convention on International Trade in Endangered Species of Wild Fauna and Flora. This program involves more than 170 countries working together to protect endangered species through worldwide control of exports and imports. The United States Fish and Wildlife Service (FWS) of the Department of the Interior is authorized to assist in the development and management of endangered species programs in foreign countries.

The IUCN, founded in 1948, is the world's largest conservation organization. It is headquartered in Gland, Switzerland. The goal of the IUCN is to promote the protection of endangered and threatened "living resources." It publishes information on endangered species worldwide in the IUCN Red List of Threatened Species.

Government Involvement in the United States

One of the earliest official recognitions of an endangered species problem in the United States was the Buffalo Protection Act of 1894. The enormous herds of buffalo that roamed through North America had been reduced to just a few individuals by the late 1800s. The law to protect the few remaining in Yellowstone National Park was the first federal legislation that focused on conserving a once-vast wildlife resource. Other national laws and regulations followed. In 1900 the Lacey Act made it illegal to import certain birds and mammals that other countries had identified as requiring protection. The National Wildlife Refuge System was started in 1903 to protect habitats that harbored fast-disappearing wildlife species. In 1940 Congress enacted the Bald Eagle Act to protect the national bird.

The Endangered Species Preservation Act of 1966 and the Endangered Species Conservation Act of 1969 demonstrated concern for disappearing species on a worldwide scale, but the laws did not directly protect the species themselves. The 1973 Endangered Species Act was the most effective and far-reaching law ever passed in the United States to protect plants and animals in natural ecosystems. The act obligates the government to protect all animal and plant life threatened with extinction, defining as threatened any species "which is likely to become endangered in the foreseeable future throughout all or a significant portion of its range." It also provides for the drawing up of lists of such species and promotes the protection of critical habitats (areas designated as critical to the survival of a species).

The Endangered Species Act is administered by the FWS and the National Marine Fisheries Service (NMFS) of the Department

of Commerce. Species are officially added to the endangered list through an established administrative process. A proposed listing of a species is published in the Federal Register. Scientists, conservationists, and government officials are asked to provide information about the biological status of the species. The FWS or NMFS accumulates the data and makes a decision about the species within the guidelines specified in the Endangered Species Act. A species may be listed as endangered or threatened, it may be removed from consideration, or more information may be required. Once a species has been listed, the FWS or NMFS develop programs to protect the remaining members of the species and return the species to a point at which it can function in a natural manner. Programs for raising some species in captivity have been carried out in attempts to restore population levels.

Private Organizations

Further aid for vanishing species comes from private organizations involved in educating the public about environmental issues. Many organizations promote species preservation through magazines, lecture series, Web sites, and television programs. In addition, many groups lobby legislators to support protection laws. Some also take more direct action. The Nature Conservancy, for example, buys and preserves tracts of habitat vital to endangered species. The World Wildlife Fund monitors the illegal trade in endangered animals and helps establish reserves for threatened wildlife, among many other projects. The primary tactic of Greenpeace has been "direct, nonviolent actions," such as steering small inflatable craft between the harpoon guns of whalers and their endangered prey.

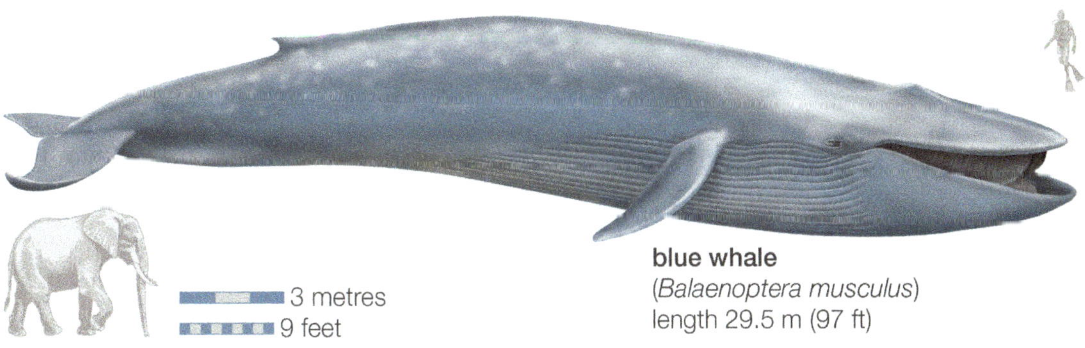

Blue whale. **Encyclopædia Britannica, Inc.**

Why Preservation?

The 1973 Endangered Species Act addressed the issue of why an endangered species of plant or animal should be offered formal protection. As stated in the act, such species "are of esthetic, ecological, educational, historical, recreational, and scientific value to the Nation and its people." Numerous species are medically or agriculturally significant because of their unique properties or traits. It cannot be predicted when a species might be discovered to be of direct value to humans. Once a species becomes extinct, any benefits it might have provided are lost forever.

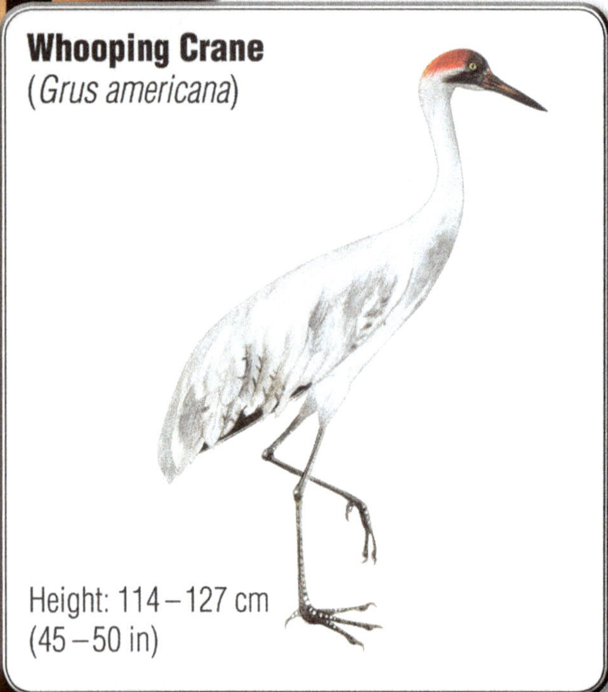

The whooping crane was on the verge of extinction in 1941–42, when only 15 or 16 of the birds remained. Conservation programs increased the population, but the bird is still endangered. Encyclopædia Britannica, Inc.

As scientists unravel the intricate network of plant-animal relationships in the natural world, more and more species are discovered to have a vital, and often unsuspected, dependence on other species. Obviously, if the extinction of one species is permitted through rapid, human-caused activities that do not permit natural adaptations and evolution to occur, certain other species may also be affected. This can result in a "domino effect" of potential extinctions.

Through breeding programs and reintroduction of animals into their natural habitats, several species have been brought back from the brink of extinction, including the black-footed ferret and the California condor, though both are still endangered. Several more species are undergoing such programs, and they will eventually be reintroduced into the wild.

CHAPTER 6
Examples of Endangered Species

The list of plant and animal species recognized as endangered or threatened is much too long to allow for discussion of each. Selected examples, however, serve to indicate the problems faced and solutions being applied.

Birds

The International Union for Conservation of Nature and Natural Resources (IUCN) lists about 500 bird species as endangered (or critically endangered) worldwide, and the United States Fish and Wildlife Service (FWS) lists more than 75 in the United States. Birds provide several modern examples of how extinction can occur. One of the best known is the passenger pigeon, a species said to have occurred in greater numbers than any other bird or mammal for which there are records. Passenger pigeons looked quite similar to mourning doves, a close relative that is still common. One distinction—a requirement for nesting in colonies—ultimately led to the downfall of the passenger pigeon. The birds, concentrated at nesting sites, were slaughtered for food by the millions. The extinction of the passenger pigeon is a commentary on the erroneous belief that if a species occurs in large numbers it is unnecessary to be concerned about its welfare. Although John James Audubon reported seeing more than 1 billion of these birds in Kentucky in 1813, the last member of the species died in 1914.

The ivory-billed woodpecker, the largest woodpecker to inhabit North America, was believed to be on the verge of extinction, if not already extinct. There were unconfirmed sightings of the bird in the southern United States in the late 1990s. In 2005 a team of researchers announced that the ivory-billed woodpecker had indeed been sighted in eastern Arkansas, though

Passenger Pigeon
(Ectopistes migratorius)

Length: 32 cm (13 in)

The passenger pigeon is now extinct. The last member of the species died in 1914. **Encyclopædia Britannica, Inc.**

The Philippine eagle is considered critically endangered. Encyclopædia Britannica, Inc.

skepticism over the rediscovery persisted among some scientists. The species' decline coincided with the logging of virgin forest, where it had subsisted on deadwood insects.

The world's last dusky seaside sparrow died in Florida in June 1987 because its habitat, Florida's coastal salt marsh, was severely depleted. Among birds outside of the United States, the Philippine eagle, the Chinese crested tern, and the Siberian crane are just a few examples of species considered critically endangered.

Insects

According to the IUCN, nearly 200 of the world's insect species are endangered. The FWS identifies more than 50 in the United States, including two butterfly species—the San Bruno elfin and the mission blue—whose populations have been reduced in size or eliminated because of urban development in the San Francisco area. The FWS recovery plan focuses primarily on conserving the few remaining habitats where the species occur. Threats to the species and their habitats include new urban development, herbicides that destroy plants on which the species depend, insecticides that kill butterflies as well as pests, off-road vehicles that destroy vegetation, and the introduction of nonnative plants that compete with native species required by butterflies. The recovery plan also provides for research programs designed to understand the requirements of each species so that proper habitat management decisions can be made.

Mission Blue Butterfly
(*Icaricia icarioides missionensis*)

Length: 1.9 – 3.2 cm (0.75 – 1.25 in)

The mission blue butterfly is an endangered insect. **Encyclopædia Britannica, Inc.**

FISHES

Worldwide nearly 1,200 species of fish have been identified as threatened with extinction. Examples of fish deemed endangered include the Asian arowana, the Chinese paddlefish, and the Nassau grouper. In the United States, many species of desert fishes became extinct before protective measures were taken. Despite laws for protection, many of the desert aquatic habitats and their associated species are still in danger. Numerous conservation groups and concerned individuals are working in cooperation with the FWS to assure more lasting protection for desert fishes through land acquisition and the passage and enforcement of stricter laws.

The largetooth sawfish is among nearly 1,200 species of fish identified as threatened with extinction. **Encyclopædia Britannica, Inc.**

REPTILES AND AMPHIBIANS

More than 1,300 species of reptiles and amphibians are recognized by the IUCN as endangered, including certain crocodiles and sea turtles. Many species have been depleted by overhunting and damage to their nesting grounds. Among the United States amphibian species listed as endangered or threatened by the FWS are the Red Hills salamander, confined to a few streamside habitats in Alabama, and the Houston toad of Texas. Listed reptile species in the United States include the desert tortoise in the Southwest, the blunt-nosed leopard lizard in California, and the eastern indigo snake in the Southeast. Outside of the

Chinese Alligator
(*Alligator sinensis*)

Length: 200 cm (79 in)

The Chinese alligator is an endangered reptile. **Encyclopædia Britannica, Inc.**

The endangered leatherback sea turtle is the largest of the living turtles. **Encyclopædia Britannica, Inc.**

United States, the Venezuelan yellow frog, the Cuban pine toad, and the Baw Baw frog of Australia number among the endangered amphibians, while endangered reptiles include the Chinese alligator and the Asian three-striped box turtle.

MAMMALS

More than 1,000 mammals of the world are threatened with extinction. These include both species of elephant, eight species of whale, and some 65 primates, as well as deer, leopards, tigers, and other large mammals whose numbers have been severely reduced by overhunting

West Indian manatee. **Encyclopædia Britannica, Inc.**

West Indian manatee
(*Trichechus manatus*)
average length 3 m (10 ft)

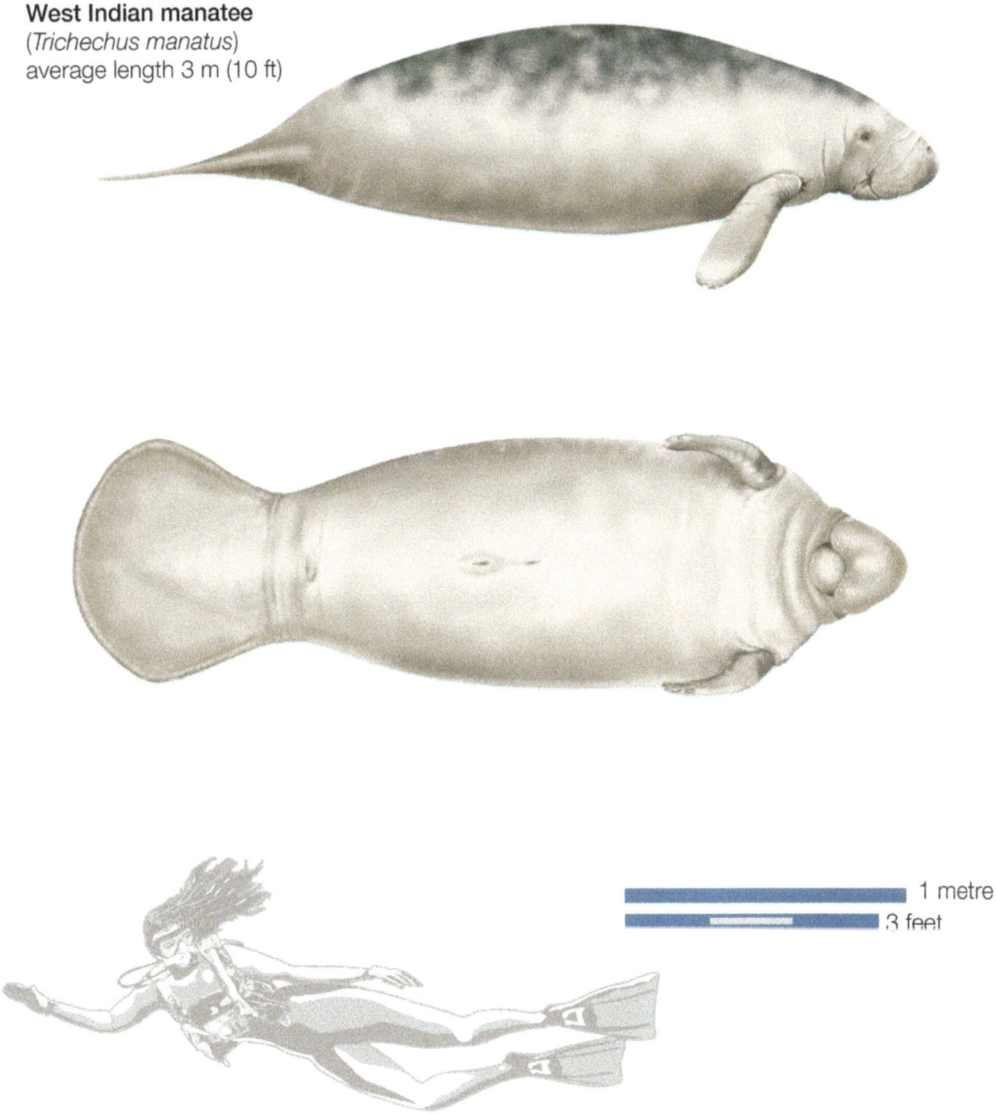

Ethiopian Wolf
(*Canis simensis*)

The Ethiopian wolf is an endangered mammal of Ethiopia's highlands.. **Encyclopædia Britannica, Inc.**

and habitat destruction. Included among United States mammals that are protected to some degree are the gray wolf, the Florida panther, and the grizzly bear.

Conclusion

By the early 21st century, the environmental movement had reached the mainstream. A growing number of people had adopted at least some aspects of a "green" lifestyle, including recycling, buying environmentally friendly products, and using public transportation. Such everyday choices by individuals play an important part in saving the environment. Ultimately, however, environmental laws are necessary to ensure that governments, corporations, and individuals act in ways that preserve the planet and protect all the species—animal, plant, and human—that inhabit it. The ongoing challenge of the environmental movement, and its allies in government, is finding compromises that are acceptable not only to its members but also to business leaders and the public at large.

Glossary

anthropocentric Interpreting or regarding the world in terms of human values and experiences.

biocentric Considering all forms of life as having intrinsic value.

deep ecology A movement or a body of concepts that considers humans no more important than other species and that advocates a corresponding radical readjustment of the relationships between humans and nature.

domino effect A cumulative effect produced when one event initiates a succession of similar events.

ecofeminism A movement or theory that applies feminist principles and ideas to ecological issues.

ecosystem An ecological unit made up of organisms and the environment they live in.

ecoterrorism The sabotage of activities that are harmful to the environment or animals, often by violent means.

erosion The process of slowly wearing away.

extinction In biology, the dying out or termination of a species.

herbicide An agent (such as a chemical) used to destroy or inhibit plant growth;

specifically, a selective weed killer that does not injure crop plants.

lobby To conduct activities with the objective of influencing public officials and especially members of a legislative body with regard to legislation and other policy decisions.

ozone A form of oxygen in which the molecule contains three atoms instead of two.

ozone layer, or ozonosphere Region in the upper atmosphere between about 9 and 22 miles (15 and 35 kilometers) in altitude, in which there are appreciable concentrations of ozone; it protects Earth by absorbing harmful ultraviolet radiation from the Sun.

pesticide An agent (such as a chemical) used to destroy pests.

recycling The recovery and reuse of materials from spent products.

reforest To renew forest cover on denuded land by natural seeding or artificial planting.

sanction A measure taken against a country that violates a law.

smelter An establishment that processes metal.

stewardship The careful, responsible management of something (such as natural resources) entrusted to one's care.

timbering The act of cutting down trees for commercial purposes.

troika Any group of three acting in unison to exert influence, control, and so forth.

For More Information

The Canadian Ecology Centre
6905 Hwy 17, P.O. Box 430
Mattawa, ON P0H 1V0
Canada
(888) 747-7577
Web site: http://www.canadianecology.ca
The Canadian Ecology Centre focuses on conservation and development issues. Hands-on activities and training in outdoor skills are also available at the center.

Conservation International
2011 Crystal Drive, Suite 500
Arlington, VA 22202
(800) 429-5660
Web site: http://www.conservation.org
Conservation International aims to protect resources and address climate, freshwater, and biodiversity issues that affect communities around the world. The site offers information on careers in fields related to conservation as well as a helpful glossary.

Environmental Protection Agency
Ariel Rios Building
1200 Pennsylvania Avenue NW
Washington, DC 20460
(202) 272-0167

Web site: http://www.epa.gov
The Environmental Protection Agency offers interactive quizzes and games to promote awareness of various ecological topics as well as project ideas for students who would like to take action on environmental issues in their own communities.

Friends of the Earth
1100 15th Street NW
11th Floor
Washington, DC 20005
(202) 783-7400
Web site: http://www.foe.org
Friends of the Earth advocates for a variety of environmental causes and offers information on issues such as global warming, clean energy, and the protection of marine ecosystems.

Greenpeace
702 H Street NW
Suite 300
Washington, DC 20001
(202) 462-1177
Web site: http://www.greenpeace.org
Using peaceful direct action, Greenpeace campaigns for environmentally

responsible behavior by pressuring governments and businesses to adopt environmentally friendly practices. The site suggests a number of steps that can be taken to promote its conservation and protection efforts.

Nature Canada
75 Albert Street Suite 300
Ottawa, ON K1P 5E7
Canada
(800) 267-4088
Web site: http://www.naturecanada.ca
The nonprofit agency Nature Canada seeks to protect wildlife and natural habitats throughout Canada. Outreach programs, publications, and volunteer support are among the means the organization uses to reach its goals.

World Wildlife Fund
1250 24th Street NW
P.O. Box 97180
Washington, DC 20090
(202) 293-4800
Web site: http://www.worldwildlife.org
The World Wildlife Fund is a global organization dedicated to protecting the planet's various ecosystems and wildlife.

The site provides information on scholarship and fellowship opportunities for students interested in becoming active in conservation efforts.

Web Sites

Due to the changing nature of Internet links, Rosen Educational Services has developed an online list of Web sites related to the subject of this book. This site is updated regularly. Please use this link to access the list:

http://www.rosenlinks.com/teos/poli

Bibliography

Archer, Jules. *To Save the Earth: The American Environmental Movement* (Viking, 1998).

Asimov, Isaac. *Why Are Animals Endangered?* (Gareth Stevens, 1993).

Barnes, Simon. *Planet Zoo: One Hundred Animals We Can't Afford to Lose* (Orion Children's, 2000).

Bright, Michael. *The Encyclopedia of Endangered and Extinct Animals* (Copper Beech Books, 2001).

Calhoun, Yael, ed. *Environmental Policy* (Chelsea House, 2005).

Connolly, Sean. *Safeguarding the Environment* (Smart Apple Media, 2006).

David, Laurie. *The Solution Is You: An Activist's Guide* (Fulcrum, 2006).

Eblen, R.A., and Eblen, W.R., eds. *The Environment Encyclopedia* (Marshall Cavendish, 2001).

Goodnough, David. *Endangered Animals of North America: A Hot Issue* (Enslow Publishers, 2001).

Halpin, Mikki. *It's Your World—If You Don't Like It, Change It: Activism for Teenagers* (Simon Pulse, 2004).

Juniper, Tony. *Saving Planet Earth* (Collins, 2007).

McDaniel, C.N. *Wisdom for a Livable Planet* (Trinity Univ. Press, 2005).

Miles, Victoria. *Wild Science: Amazing Encounters Between Animals and the People Who Study Them* (Raincoast Books, 2004).

Sonneborn, Liz. *The Environmental Movement* (Chelsea House, 2007).

Switzer, J.V. *Environmental Activism: A Reference Handbook* (ABC-CLIO, 2003).

U.S. Dept. of the Interior. *Endangered and Threatened Wildlife and Plants* (U.S. Fish and Wildlife Service, annual).

Weyler, Rex. *Greenpeace* (Rodale, 2004).

D

E

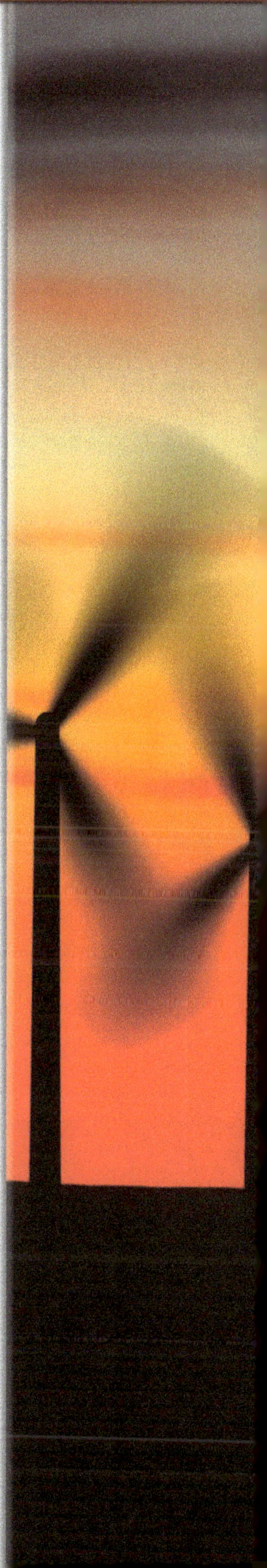

O

P

R

S

T

U